# DEAR MOUSE FRIENDS, WELCOME TO THE

# WELCOME TO THE STONE AGE . . . AND THE WORLD OF THE CAVEMICE!

**CAPITAL:** OLD MOUSE CITY

**POPULATION:** WE'RE NOT SURE. (MATH DOESN'T EXIST YET!) BUT BESIDES CAVEMICE, THERE ARE PLENTY OF DINOSAURS, <u>WAY</u> TOO MANY SABER-TOOTHED TIGERS, AND FEROCIOUS CAVE BEARS — BUT NO MOUSE HAS EVER HAD THE COURAGE TO COUNT THEM!

**TYPICAL FOOD:** PETRIFIED CHEESE SOUP

**NATIONAL HOLIDAY:** **GREAT ZAP DAY**, WHICH CELEBRATES THE DISCOVERY OF FIRE. RODENTS EXCHANGE GRILLED CHEESE SANDWICHES ON THIS HOLIDAY.

**NATIONAL DRINK:** MAMMOTH MILKSHAKES

**CLIMATE:** Unpredictable, WITH FREQUENT METEOR SHOWERS

cheese soup

milkshake

## MONEY

SEASHELLS OF ALL SHAPES AND SIZES

## MEASUREMENT

THE BASIC UNIT OF MEASUREMENT IS BASED ON THE LENGTH OF THE TAIL OF THE LEADER OF THE VILLAGE. A UNIT CAN BE DIVIDED INTO A HALF TAIL OR QUARTER TAIL. THE LEADER IS ALWAYS READY TO PRESENT HIS TAIL WHEN THERE IS A DISPUTE.

# THE CAVEMICE

Geronimo

Trap

Thea

Benjamin

Bugsy Wugsy

Hercule Poirat

Grandma Ratrock

# CAVEMICE

# SEA MONSTER SURPRISE!

Scholastic Inc.

Copyright © 2013 by Edizioni Piemme S.p.A., Palazzo Mondadori, Via Mondadori 1, 20090 Segrate, Italy. International Rights © Atlantyca S.p.A. English translation © 2016 by Atlantyca S.p.A.

The publisher does not have any control over and does not assume any responsibility for author or third-party websites or their content.

GERONIMO STILTON names, characters, and related indicia are copyright, trademark, and exclusive license of Atlantyca S.p.A. All rights reserved. The moral right of the author has been asserted. Based on an original idea by Elisabetta Dami. www.geronimostilton.com

Published by Scholastic Inc., *Publishers since 1920*, 557 Broadway, New York, NY 10012. SCHOLASTIC and associated logos are trademarks and/or registered trademarks of Scholastic Inc.

*Stilton is the name of a famous English cheese. It is a registered trademark of the Stilton Cheese Makers' Association. For more information, go to www.stiltoncheese.com.*

No part of this publication may be reproduced, stored in a retrieval system, or transmitted in any form or by any means, electronic, mechanical, photocopying, recording, or otherwise, without written permission of the copyright holder. For information regarding permission, please contact: Atlantyca S.p.A., Via Leopardi 8, 20123 Milan, Italy; e-mail foreignrights@atlantyca.it, www.atlantyca.com.

This book is a work of fiction. Names, characters, places, and incidents are either the product of the author's imagination or are used fictitiously, and any resemblance to actual persons, living or dead, business establishments, events, or locales is entirely coincidental.

ISBN 978-0-545-87248-5

Text by Geronimo Stilton
Original title *Polposaura affamata . . . coda stritolata!*
Cover by Flavio Ferron
Illustrations by Giuseppe Facciotto (design) and Alessandro Costa (color)
Graphics by Marta Lorini and Chiara Cebraro

Special thanks to Tracey West
Translated by Andrea Schaffer
Interior design by Becky James

10 9 8 7 6 5 4 3 2 1                          16 17 18 19 20

Printed in the U.S.A.                                          40
First printing 2016

MANY AGES AGO, ON PREHISTORIC MOUSE ISLAND, THERE WAS A VILLAGE CALLED OLD MOUSE CITY. IT WAS INHABITED BY BRAVE *RODENT SAPIENS* KNOWN AS THE CAVEMICE.

DANGERS SURROUNDED THE MICE AT EVERY TURN: EARTHQUAKES, METEOR SHOWERS, FEROCIOUS DINOSAURS, AND FIERCE GANGS OF SABER-TOOTHED TIGERS. BUT THE BRAVE CAVEMICE FACED IT ALL WITH A SENSE OF HUMOR, AND WERE ALWAYS READY TO LEND A HAND TO OTHERS.

HOW DO I KNOW THIS? I DISCOVERED AN ANCIENT BOOK WRITTEN BY MY ANCESTOR, GERONIMO STILTONOOT! HE CARVED HIS STORIES INTO STONE TABLETS AND ILLUSTRATED THEM WITH HIS ETCHINGS.

I AM PROUD TO SHARE THESE STONE AGE STORIES WITH YOU. THE EXCITING ADVENTURES OF THE CAVEMICE WILL MAKE YOUR FUR STAND ON END, AND THE JOKES WILL TICKLE YOUR WHISKERS! HAPPY READING!

*Geronimo Stilton*

WARNING! DON'T IMITATE THE CAVEMICE. WE'RE NOT IN THE STONE AGE ANYMORE!

# BON VOYAGE, BART BARNACLE!

It was a beautiful spring morning. The sky was blue, the sun shone brightly, and the air was CLEAR and as crisp as a cheese cracker.

I was about to witness a historic (I mean, *pre*historic) moment. Bart Barnacle, brave pirate and friend to cavemice, was about to sail home to Black Rock Island in the Land of the Rising Sun.

All the furry citizens of Old Mouse City gathered at the port to wish him a safe trip.

Sorry, I haven't introduced myself yet! I am Stiltonoot, Geronimo Stiltonoot, and I am the editor of *The Stone Gazette*, the most famouse newspaper in prehistory (maybe because it's the only one!).

Anyway, as I was saying, Bart was headed to the Land of the Rising Sun. It is a group of islands far, far away and is home to the PREHISTORIC PIRATES. To go there, you must sail in the direction that the sun rises.

The trip takes a LOOOOOONG, LOOOOOONG time. You could age a wheel of

Ahoy!

cheddar while you're waiting to get there.

Speaking of **cheese**, Bart had plenty stashed on his boat! He had built a **STURDY** pirate ship while he was here. (At the same time, he taught us how to build ships, too. We just still had to learn how to **sail** them!)

Now, where was I? Oh, yes. My cousin Trap and I were headed to Bart's **CAVE** to escort him to the port. We were almost there when . . .

"**HEY!** Why are you two up so early?"

**GREAT ROCKY BOULDERS! IT SOUNDED LIKE . . . BUT IT COULDN'T BE . . .**

It was my friend Hercule Poirat, the most famouse detective in the **STONE AGE**!

"Bart Barnacle is sailing home," I told him.

"And we are bringing him to the port," added Trap.

4

## "BONES AND STONES!"

exclaimed Hercule. "I would come, too, but I'm on my way to solve a mystery in **Thickrock Village**. I'm running late."

"Good luck!" I said.

"**THANKS, FRIENDS!**" said Hercule.

I'm late!

"Please tell Bart Barnacle that I wish him a safe trip."

Hercule scampered off, and Trap and I arrived at the cave of our **pirate** friend.

"**Good morning**," he greeted us. "I wish we could sit and chat one last time, but we have to get *MOVING*. There's a long voyage ahead of me!"

We walked to the port, where a **crowd of cavemice** had already gathered. Some of them were wiping away TEARS. Everyone loved Bart Barnacle — he was such an amazing mouse!

He had impressed us by building such a BIG — no, HUGE — no, ENORMOUSE ship! Bart had named it the *Speedy Cheddar 3*. (The *Speedy Cheddar* and *Speedy Cheddar 2* hadn't turned out so well. They had both

**sank** as soon as they were on the water. But the **SPEEDY CHEDDAR 3** was in much better shape.)

"Bon voyage, Bart!" called out my nephew Benjamin. "Say hi to everyone on Black Rock Island for us."

"COME AND SEE US AGAIN SOON!" said my sister, Thea.

"And bring back some of those tasty noodles they make there!" Trap added.

"GOOD-BYE, FRIENDS!" Bart called back. He started to walk up the gangway. And then . . .

**WAAAAAAHHH!**

Bart S**T⊙PPED** on the gangway. He stood as still as a block of **cheese**.

We stared at him, wondering what was happening. Suddenly, he burst into TEARS!

**BOUNCING BOULDERS –** they weren't just tears. He was crying a waterfall!

"WAAAAAAHHH!" he sobbed. "I don't want to leave you, friends."

We were *squeakless*. Bart Barnacle didn't

want to leave because we meant **SO MUCH** to him!

"But all your friends on Black Rock Island are waiting for you," Benjamin encouraged him.

"And so is your grandfather **BLACKBEARD BARNACLE**!" said Thea.

"You can come back to Old Mouse City whenever you want," I told Bart. "But now that you have built this giant **pirate ship**, it's time to set sail!"

Bart blew his snout. "Sniff! It's true. The *Speedy Cheddar 3* is a fine vessel. I can't let it stay tied to the dock like a mussel **CLINGING** to a rock." Then he brightened. "I have a solution! You, my friends, can all *come with me*!"

I quickly raised my 🐾🐾🐾 to get his attention. "I'm sorry, but I can't—"

Then I heard the booming voice of our village leader, **ErneSt HeftymouSe**.

"Good for you, Stiltonoot!" he cried. "You bravely raised your paw to VOLUÏTEER to accompany Bart Barnacle on his long journey to the **Land of the Rising Sun!**"

Everyone applauded.

"Grandson, **how brave**!" called out Grandma Ratrock. "Just like your grandma!"

"**Very brave** indeed," said Bluster Conjurat, our village shaman. "Who would have guessed?"

"Bravo, Stiltonoot!" cheered **LEO EDISTONE**, the brilliant inventor.

"Um, but I — um, I didn't VOLUÏTEER," I tried to protest.

"**You're amazing, Uncle!**" exclaimed Benjamin. "Can I come with you?"

"I want to go, too!" added Thea. "Bart can

12

teach me to **navigate** the seas."

Grandma Ratrock chimed in. "Some life at sea will do you good, Grandson."

"**ARE YOU JOKING?**" I asked. "The ocean is filled with dangers. **We will all go extinct!**"

I was not going to change my mind. Nothing could move me. Zero. Zilch.

"What a good friend you are, Geronimo. Always so helpful."

Bouncing boulders! The mouse who said that was . . . but it couldn't be . . .

"Cl-Clarissa?" I stuttered.

I turned and found myself looking at Clarissa Conjurat, the mouse of my **dreams**.

I stared into her **EYES** for a moment. They were the color of **BLUE CHEESE**. Her lashes were as long as . . .

"It's very **brave** of you to do this, Geronimo," Clarissa said. "You'll be facing storms, hurricanes, high winds, hungry sea monsters . . ."

You're so brave!

TAP TAP

GULP

"St-storms? H-hurricanes? H-high winds?" I stuttered. "And **HUNGRY SEA MONSTERS**?"

Grandma Ratrock

slapped me on the back. "Isn't my grandson the most COURAGEOUS journalist you've ever met?" she asked proudly.

Clarissa **smiled**, and I knew I was sunk. I could not back down now.

I had to journey the seas with Bart Barnacle!

# A DINNER FIT FOR A DINOSAUR!

Grandma Ratrock decided that Bart's ship would **DEPART** the next morning at dawn — with Thea, Trap, Benjamin, and me on board.

"Couldn't we leave at noon?" Trap asked with a long **YAAAAWN**.

"Or two? Or three? Or never?" I suggested.

But Grandma was more stubborn than a **BOULDER**, more solid than a **GRANITE** wall, and more determined than a charging **MaMMOtH**.

"**NO EXCUSES!**" she said firmly. "This trip will make you all as sharp as cheddar!"

"Why aren't you going, Grandma?" I asked.

"Because I'm **SHARP ENOUGH** already!" she snapped (and that certainly was true).

I sighed.

## Petrified cheese!

There was nothing left to do but **run** back to my cave and pack my bags. I had no idea what to expect in the **Land of the Rising Sun**, so I packed everything I could think of. I started with my favorite pillow. I like to be **comfy** when I sleep!

*Puff! Pant!*

Then I packed my clothes: my *heavy* winter loincloth, my

LIGHT spring loincloth, my fancy loincloth for special events, and lots of extra underwear. Finally, I added a hot water bottle to help me in case I got a tummyache on the high seas.

## Fossilized feta!

My bag was so stuffed that I could barely close it! I PUSHED and puffed and panted until finally I tied it shut. By then, I was hungry, so I was glad that it was time to eat. Trap had invited us to the Rotten Tooth Tavern for a

BUUUPP!

dinner in honor of Bart Barnacle.

The pirate had an appetite as **BIG** as his ship! In just a few minutes, he devoured a pot of **stew**, a cheese **omelet** (made from pterodactyl eggs), a basket of cheddar **biscuits**, and a megalithic roast of **MEAT**!

To be honest, Trap, Benjamin, and I stuffed ourselves, too.

**BURP!**

"Watch out, or you'll get a stomachache," Thea warned.

Thea was right, but I couldn't help myself. Trap almost never offers me food for **FREE**!

To show my gratitude, I stayed to help Trap **clean up**. I was clearing dirty dishes off the tables when . . .

"**Psst, Ger!**" whispered Trap. "Two thieves are walking off with the leftovers in the kitchen!"

"What? Are you sure?" I whispered back.

He took my paw and then, as quiet as a rat at a cat party, he led me to the **D A R K** kitchen.

It was so dark that I couldn't see my WHISKERS in front of my face.

Then Trap lit a TORCH, and we could see two **LARGE**, **DARK**, **FURRY** shadows!

"Heeeeelp!" I shrieked.

"**WHO ARE YOU?**" Trap yelled in a threatening tone.

Quick as **lightning**, the shadows dashed off. Trap went after them, but he TRIPPED over a bowl . . .

CRAAAAAASH!

By the time we caught up to the thieves, they were diving into the *WATER*!

We *RACED* to Thea's cave and told her what happened.

"I think the thieves were saber-toothed tigers!" I said. "They were big and furry!"

Thea shook her head. "What would **TIGERS** be doing in the tavern? It sounds like you were having a **NIGHTMARE**. Go back to bed."

Look!

I see!

SPLASH

SPLASH

"But I wasn't **sleeping**," I protested.

"Maybe Thea's right," Trap said. "It's late, we're *tired*, and we might have been seeing things. Let's get some sleep."

So I went home and fell asleep — but I dreamed all night of fanged cats ready to gobble me up for a **midnight snack**!

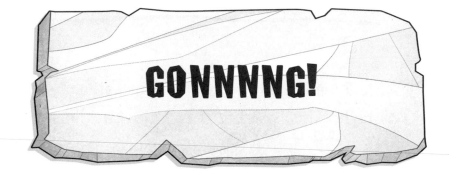

**GONNNNG!**

At dawn, a loud noise jolted me out of bed.

# GONNNNG!

"What's happening?" I cried. "Did the **CHEDDAR VOLCANO** erupt? Is it an earthquake? A **meteorite crash**?"

But it was not a natural disaster.

"**GET OUT OF BED, LAZYBONES!**" a voice yelled.

I sighed. It was Grandma Ratrock, using the village **GONG** to wake us up!

Grandma kept **BANGING** the gong until I came out of my cave and Thea, Trap, and

Benjamin came out of theirs.

"Look sharp, **SLEEPYHEADS**!" she demanded. "Tails up, **EYES** open, and WHiSKeRS straight! And when you get to Black Rock Island, behave yourselves! Say please and thank you and don't act like **cheeseheads**! Make Old Mouse City proud!"

We CARRIED our bags on board the *Speedy Cheddar 3*.

I thought I had the **HEAVIEST** bag in all of prehistory, but Thea had me beat.

"What . . . HUFF . . . is inside . . .
PUFF . . . this trunk?" Bart Barnacle
snorted as he carried it up the gangplank.

"Just what's necessary," Thea replied.
"You never know what we might encounter."

"Like what?" I asked.

"**Mountains** or *beaches* or
**volcanoes** or **snow**," Thea replied. "I
need the right gear for any environment!"

Trap, meanwhile, had packed a bag

Let's go!

Oof!

full of **cheese**. Only Benjamin had a lightweight backpack with just the essentials.

When we were all aboard, the citizens of Old Mouse City called out their good-byes.

## "HAVE A SAFE TRIP!"

## "WATCH OUT FOR SEA MONSTERS!"

### "Did you remember to make a will?"

"If you don't come back, I get Geronimo's cave!" exclaimed Grandma Ratrock.

"And I get Trap's supply of **cheddar**!" said Bluster Conjurat.

Wasn't the crowd supposed to be encouraging us? They weren't doing a very good job!

Luckily, it was time to leave. Bart Barnacle

was ready to train us to become the CREW of his **pirate ship**.

"The **anchor** keeps the boat from drifting away," he explained. Then he handed us the end of a thick rope. "On the count of three, PULL with all your might. One . . . two . . . THREE!"

We YANKED on the rope, and the anchor, carved from solid granite, came unstuck! Not only that, but it SPLASHED out of the water, swung in the air, and landed right on the top of my furry head!

# GONNNNG!

"Ha, ha! Cousin, your head rang like Grandma Ratrock's GONG!" Trap teased.

"Funny," I mumbled, rubbing the dino-

egg-sized **bump** on my head.

It was a sign; I was sure of it. A sign that we were headed for a **sea of trouble**!

Ooooooooooow!

# LEARNING THE ROPES

Bart Barnacle was an **expert sailor**, and he tried very hard to turn us into an EXPERT CREW.

But that wasn't an easy task!

Um . . .

To your posts!

As soon as the *Speedy Cheddar 3* left the port, he called for our attention.

"Now we will learn how to **set the sails**!" he announced. He climbed up a rope ladder leading to the tall pole that was the main mast. "**WATCH ME** and do as I do!"

I looked up. The mast seemed to touch the clouds!

We're ready!

Yes!

"Do we have to climb up there?" I asked. "Isn't there an *easier* way?"

"This is the **only** way," Bart replied. "Do as I say and everything will be fine!"

*Oops...*

So we climbed up after him. The ladder *jiggled* like Jurassic jelly with each step we took.

"It's so **shaky**!" Trap wailed.

*Squeak!*

"Just climb with **CONFIDENCE**," Thea said as she quickly climbed up the set of ropes across from us.

Benjamin was right behind

her. "This is FUN, Uncle Ger!"

The ropes I was climbing were shaking so hard I thought I might fall off! I closed my eyes.

When I opened them, Thea and Benjamin had already reached the sails. They each untied a rope attached to a sail. Then they gracefully swung back down to the deck, unfurling the sails as they went.

"We have to do THAT?" I asked nervously.

"Just reach up and loosen the knots!" Bart called. "Then swing down."

Trap loosened the knot just above his head. He gripped the rope and tried to swing down.

"Whoaaa!" Trap shrieked. The rope twirled, wrapping around him. He was dangling from the mast like a fish on a line!

33

"Maybe I should just climb down," I suggested.

"You can do it, Uncle Ger!" Benjamin cheered me on. "Just pull the rope."

I didn't want to disappoint him. With a gulp, I pulled it.

# FRUUUSSSHHHHHHHH!

The sail quickly unraveled. I clung to the rope as tightly as I could and slid down toward the deck. Before I could breathe a sigh of relief . . .

"LOOK OUT! FIRE!" yelled Benjamin.

Oh no! The rope I was on was starting to catch FIRE!

"Aaaaahhhhh!" I squealed.

"The FRICTION of Geronimo's fur against the rope is causing it to burn!" Bart called out.

Aaaaahhhhh!

Trap threw a bucket of water on me.
**Splash!**
I was safe but **WET**. This trip was
getting off to a terrible start!

# AS GREEN AS MOLDY CHEESE!

With our sails blowing in the wind, the *Speedy Cheddar 3* set out to sea. Destination: **the Land of the Rising Sun!**

For the first few days, the voyage went smoothly. The **waves** were gentle, the **WIND** was strong, and the **weather** was warm and clear.

Benjamin and Thea were having fun. Bart taught them how to use the **helm**.*

On the other paw, I was not having fun. The waves made me **seasick**. The strong winds made me **seasick**. Even the warm weather made me **seasick**!

* The helm is the wheel used to steer the ship.

My complexion was as green as moldy cheese! But I wasn't the only one who was having trouble. Trap was strangely quiet, and he wasn't eating!

"Are you seasick, Uncle Trap?" Benjamin asked.

"Maybe it's just indigestion," he said. "BURP!"

"That makes sense," said my nephew.

Hmm...

Burp!

"The pantry is almost EMPTY. If you ate all those snacks, it's no wonder you're sick."

"That wasn't me!" Trap protested. "I didn't eat EVERYThiNG in the pantry. Just a hunk of smoked cheddar. And a dozen MOZZARELLA STICKS. And a cheesecake. But that was TWO DAYS ago!"

Thea put her paws on her hips. "Oh, yeah? Then what happened to all the rest of the food in there? Did it JUMP into the ocean?"

"I swear, I haven't eaten in TWO DAYS!" Trap insisted.

"Well, if it's indigestion you have, my friend, then I know a great cure," said Bart.

Trap brightened.

"When I feel sick, I clean!" Bart said cheerfully.

Trap groaned. "I **WASH**, I **DUST**, and I **polish**," Bart went on. "I scrub the ship from top to bottom until I'm feeling better."

Trap rubbed his **belly**. "Thinking about **cleaning**

1 I wash ...

2 I dust ...

3 and I polish!

just makes my stomach hurt more!"

"There must be something else you can do to feel better," Thea said. "Could you take a walk? Read? Sing?"

"**THAT'S IT!**" cried Bart.

The pirate *DASHED* belowdecks and came back carrying a stringed instrument.

"This instrument is called a **MANDOLIN**," he explained. He began to **strum** the strings. "You play it like this."

A light, **delicate** tune came from the instrument.

"Thanks, friend," said Trap, taking the mandolin from Bart's paws. "I really am in the **mood** to sing something."

Trap opened his mouth wide, and a **SOUND** came out . . . a sound like a

# **WALRUSAURUS** with a sore throat!

# GREAT ROCKY BOULDERS!

It was Jurassically awful!

# UNDERWATER ATTACK!

Trap's singing did not help my seasickness. I felt **terrible**! But the worst hadn't happened yet . . .

The next morning, the water began to **foam**. The waves began to swell. Benjamin, who was acting as lookout in the crow's nest on top of the mast, shouted out:

"Sea monster on the port side!"*

Trap stopped singing. Bart, Thea, and I ran to the port side of the deck and **LOOKED** out into the water. We couldn't see a thing!

"Are you sure, Benjamin?" I yelled up to him.

* The port side is the left side of the ship when facing the front.

## "Down there! Down there!"

he yelled, pointing to the water.

Suddenly, we could all feel the boat RISING UP from the water. Before we could react . . .

SWOOOOOSHHHHH!

Look!

The *Speedy Cheddar 3* leaned way on its side. Something was **UNDERNEATH** us, pushing us up!

We looked down into the water.

Thundering triceratops! Benjamin was right. An

**enoRMouse** sea serpent stared at us with two terrifying eyes. Its body was *long* and green. Huge, **SHARP** teeth stuck out of its massive jaws.

Its long tail was lifting the boat!

Bart ran into the cabin to get the longeye* and pointed it directly at the **SEA MONSTER**.

*The longeye is the prehistoric telescope developed by Leo Edistone, the inventor from Old Mouse City.

"It's a **SERPENTSAURUS**!" he cried. "This is bad news!"

"Will it eat us?" I asked.

"It won't eat rodents, but this type of sea monster loves to eat **WOOD** and **fabric**," Bart explained. "We've got to get away from it before it **gobbles** up our ship and we're lost at sea!"

Bart raced to the helm and turned the wheel with all his might, changing the **DIRECTION** of the ship. Thea and Benjamin **scurried** to set the sails.

We got **lucky**! The **WIND** caught the sails and pushed us away from the serpentsaurus.

Trap became bold. "Hey there, **chubby**!" he called out. "It wouldn't hurt you to skip a meal, would it?"

Then the wind **died**. The serpentsaurus

* The bow is the front of a ship.

swam toward us with an **ANGRY** gleam in its eyes.

The sea monster lashed out at the *Speedy Cheddar 3*. It opened its massive jaw and . . . **CRUNCH!** It chewed off a chunk of the bow!*

"**AAAAAH!**" I yelled.

"I didn't mean it!" Trap called to the monster.

But the serpentsaurus did not accept Trap's apology.

**CRUNCH!** The serpentsaurus bit off a chunk of railing. Then it started **munching** on the sails.

Bones and stones, we were done for — doomed — **EXTINCT**!

But just when we were about to lose **HOPE**, Bart got an idea.

"Leave it to me," he announced, and then he dashed off.

He came back **dragging** Thea's heavy travel trunk.

"What are you doing with that?" she asked.

"If we give it your **clothes** to eat . . .

*huff!* . . . the monster will leave the ship alone . . . *puff!*" Bart explained. He opened the **trunk** and began to throw her gear into the water.

"My snowsuit! My raincoat! My beach towel!" she moaned. "**NOoooooo!**"

**CHOMP! CHOMP! CHOMP!**

The serpentsaurus **greedily** gobbled up each piece.

"It's working!" I cried.

Thea ran downstairs and came back holding . . . *my travel bag*!

"Take this, too," she said, thrusting it into Bart's paws.

"**NOoooooo!**" I shrieked. "My underwear! My water bottle! My best loincloth!"

The **SERPENTSAURUS** began to float on its back, leisurely munching on my clothes. (UGH!) But at least it had stopped eating our ship!

CHOMP! CHOMP! CHOMP!

Bouncing boulders, we were saved! But now we had no luggage or changes of clothes.

# OCTOSAURUS ALERT!

The *Speedy Cheddar 3* continued its journey. It had lost two **sails** and the bow and railing had some chunks bitten off, but all in all it was in good shape.

By **sunset**, things had calmed down. Bones and stones, we were **tired**! Thea and Trap straightened up the cabins. Bart stayed by the captain's wheel, on **alert** for danger. Benjamin and I **curled up** by a coil of rope.

"What a day," I said, **YAWNING**. "And soon we will arrive on Black Rock Island. **Zzzzzz!**"

I had just **dozed off** when I felt

something tickle my back.

"Benjamin, you know I'm ticklish," I mumbled sleepily.

Benjamin YAWNED. "I didn't touch you, Uncle Ger!"

If it wasn't Benjamin, then who was it? I opened my eyes.

AAAAAAAH!

A giant purple tentacle was poking out of the sea, tickling me! It was attached to a huge CREATURE with a bulbous head and two enormouse EYES!

Ha, ha, ha!

# "OCTOSAURUS ALERT!"

Bart yelled. "Save your fur!"

I tried to jump up, but I couldn't. The tentacle was wrapped around me!

# BY THE GREAT ZAP, IT WAS GOING TO SQUEEZE ME LIKE A LEMON!

Thea ran out on deck. "Free yourself, Ger!" she called out.

# HOW WAS I SUPPOSED TO DO THAT?!

The octosaurus had no intention of letting me go. And to make things **WORSE**, it began wrapping its other tentacles around the ship! The *Speedy Cheddar 3* started to SLOW DOWN.

"We're doomed!" I cried.

"WE NEED A PLAN!" Thea yelled.

"The octosaurus is even more **DANGEROUS** than the serpentsaurus," said Bart. "We've got to get out of here, fast!"

Thea's eyes lit up. "I know!"

Thea raced below the deck. We heard loud noises.

## OCTOSAURUS

NAME: OCTOSAURUS

HABITAT: THE DEEPEST PARTS OF THE OCEAN

DESCRIPTION: SHORT-TEMPERED, SOLITARY, AND A LITTLE SLIMY

EATING HABITS: IT MOSTLY EATS PLANKTON AND ALGAE, BUT ITS FAVORITE DISH IS CAVEMOUSE MEATBALLS.

IF YOU SEE ONE: GET FAR, FAR AWAY AS FAST AS YOU CAN, AND TRY NOT TO MAKE IT ANGRY!

# THUMP! CRACK! CRAAAAAAAAAASH!

She came back with her arms full of **SPLINTERED** wood.

"I broke up the furniture in our cabins," she explained. "Trap, help me light a **FIRE**!"

Thea and Trap heaped the wood on the ship's deck. My sister took a piece of flint and an iron rock and struck them together. They **SPARKED**, and then the wood caught fire.

A cloud of **smoke** wafted up from the flames.

The octosaurus began to cough. Its eyes teared up.

## COUGH! COUGH! COUGH!

Then it began to **slowly, slowly** loosen its grip, until only I remained a prisoner in its tentacles. BONES AND STONES, why does everything happen to me?

"Um, could you please Let me go?" I asked.

Then the tentacle holding me passed over the blazing fire. I *BURNED* my tail!

"Owwww, what a Paleolithic pain!" I wailed.

The FLAME singed the octosaurus, too. The tentacle loosened — right above the fire! I saw my furry life flash before my eyes.

"NOOO, DON'T LET ME FALL!" I wailed. "NOT NOOOOOW!"

What other rodent in the prehistoric world could be in danger of **BURNING UP** in the middle of the **sea**? Only me!

Then I felt someone pull my tail and . . .

# OWWWWW!

It was Bart Barnacle! He caught me in his arms.

## BOUNCING BOULDERS, THE PIRATE HAD SAVED ME!

The octosaurus swam away. When we couldn't see it anymore, Thea put out the fire. We continued to sail toward **Black Rock Island**.

Whew! Once again, we escaped extinction by a whisker!

# LAND HO!

When **NIGHT** fell, we settled down to sleep on the deck. Our cabins were a mess of **SPLINTERS** after Thea had chopped up the furniture to make a fire.

We didn't mind sleeping outside. Bright stars shone in the clear sky. It was a **MAGICAL** night.

Trap decided to add to the mood by **singing** us a song and strumming on the mandolin.

### "I beat two monsters with courage and ease, Now I deserve a big chunk of good cheese!"

"Enough!" I burst out. "Trap, don't you think of anything besides food?"

Trap thought about it. "No!"

Shaking my head, I plugged my ears with cheese cubes so I could fall asleep. I was awakened hours later by Benjamin yelling from the **crow's nest.**

### "Land ho!"

Bart looked through his longeye. "He's right! That's **Black Rock Island** up ahead! I'm home!"

We all moved to the bow to look. We saw the island in the distance — and then we saw a **dark shadow** moving toward us under the water!

"Oh no! Another monster!" Thea cried.

"Not another octosaurus!" I exclaimed.

"NO, NO, NO!" Bart replied. "Stay calm. That's not a monster. Well, it is, but it isn't."

"Do you feel okay, Bart?" Trap asked. "You seem a little confused."

"I'm fine!" Bart replied. "What I mean is, **Spotty** is a monster, but he's friendly. He's the GUARDIAN of Black Rock Island."

Just then a happy creature jumped out of the sea, splashing water all over the ship's deck.

"WONK! WONK! WONK!" he cried, clapping his fins together.

He was a Jurassic walrusaurus with a big snout and SP◎+S on his smooth skin (which I guess is how he got his name).

Spotty swam to the stern* of the ship and gave us a *BIG PUSH* with his tail. It propelled us right to the shore!

A group of **PREHISTORIC PIRATES** waited for us on the beach.

They all wore **colorful** clothing. The biggest one wore an eye patch. Each one of them had a **MUSTACHE** or beard and wore a bandanna on his head.

Bones and stones, they were pirates, all right!

WONK WONK

SLAP SLAP

*The stern is the back of the ship.

"Shiver me whiskers! Look who it is!" one of them cried.

"Bart Barnacle! Where have you been?" asked another.

One of the pirates pointed at us. "Who are these scalawags with you?" he asked. "They look too PALE and puny to be pirates!"

An impressive-looking pirate pushed his way through the group.

"Let me introduce our leader, my grandfather BLACKBEARD BARNACLE," Bart said proudly.

Ooh...

I'm back, friends!

Blackbeard approached us and shook my paw. What a grip! He nearly crushed my paw. But it was a **friendly** pawshake, just the same.

"Any friends of my grandson are friends of mine!" Blackbeard **BOOMED** in a powerful voice.

**Startled**, I jumped up, and he caught me in his arms.

"Welcome!" he said, **hugging** me tightly.

Ahoy!

Look who it is!

Welcome back!

"Er, thanks, Blackbeard," I said. "I mean, *Captain* Blackbeard."

Squeak! That was a **CLOSE ONE**. I didn't want to disrespect the pirate captain. Even though he was friendly, he was still a pirate!

# BLACKBEARD BARNACLE
## CAPTAIN OF BLACK ROCK ISLAND

**NAME:**
CAPTAIN BLACKBEARD
BARNACLE

**OCCUPATION:**
LEADER OF THE
PREHISTORIC
PIRATES

**PERSONALITY:**
SPEAKS LOUDLY
AND FORCEFULLY

**HOBBIES:**
GARDENING, COOKING,
AND CROCHETING (HE MIGHT BE A PIRATE,
BUT HE HAS A DOMESTIC SIDE, TOO!)

# WELCOME TO BLACK ROCK ISLAND

The VILLAGE of the prehistoric pirates wasn't far from the beach. The pirates provided us with four **DINOSAURS**, and we rode on their backs to get there. We had a **TOUR** of the island as we traveled.

It was **enchanting**! Tall palm trees towered over us, dripping with **sweet** and **JUICY** dates. Colorful flowers grew all around us. A fresh breeze blew in from the sea. And at the top of the hill waved the pirates' **Flag**.

Then the dinosaurs carried us across a plain full of **TALL STONES**.

"These are the menhir* of the

* A menhir, or standing stone, is a large, upright stone planted into the ground, usually of prehistoric origin.

**ancient** prehistoric pirates!" Blackbeard boomed.

I climbed off my dinosaur to get a *CLOSER* look. "They're so tall," I remarked.

"**Yes, they are!**" agreed Blackbeard enthusiastically.

His voice was so **STRONG** that it caused a piece of the stone to **crumble** and hit me on the head!

BONK

Owwww!

# WHAT A PALEOLITHIC PAIN!

Bart clapped. "You are **LUCKY**, Geronimo! The largest menhir on the island has welcomed you."

"Lucky me," I said, rubbing my **SORE** snout.

Then we passed between two rows of **GIGANTIC STATUES**.

"These are my *ancestors*, the earliest pirate captains," Blackbeard explained.

I went to get a closer look again. This time,

**BONK**

Argh!

I **tripped** on a rock and bumped into one of the statues.

OUCH! OUCH! OUCH!

"So, do you like our island?" asked Bart, smiling.

"Um, well . . ." I began, rubbing the newest **bump** on my head. "This tour is giving me a **big headache**!"

"Oh, I have the best cure for headaches," said Bart. "A dinosaur race!"

"Er . . . um, how is a RACE going to make me feel better?" I asked. But Bart pulled me back up onto a dinosaur.

"READY, SET, GO!" he yelled.

The dinosaurs CHARGED forward, racing toward the pirate village. My stomach lurched.

"**Noooo!**" I wailed. "I'd rather have a headache!"

The dinosaurs skidded to a stop when we reached the pirate village.

All the prehistoric pirates came out of their tents to greet **Bart Barnacle**.

"When did you get back? What have you brought? Where did you put the loot?" everyone asked at once.

Bart motioned to us. "I have brought the most precious loot of all . . . my friends!"

The pirates clapped, and Bart brought us inside the village **PANTRY**.

Petrified provolone! It held a MOUNTAIN of food: baskets of tropical fruit, barrels of buns, platters of pastries, and stacks and

stacks of **stinky cheese**!

As Bart gave us a tour of the village, the friendly pirates prepared a great **FEAST** for us. They set up the BANQUET at a long table, and soon we were all squeaking and laughing. Then Trap began to strum the mandolin and sing:

**"NOBODY THROWS A FEAST LIKE OUR PIRATE FRIENDS, LET'S DANCE AND EAT UNTIL THE NIGHT ENDS!"**

Bravo!

CLAP

CLAP

CLAP

CLAP CLAP

We jumped up and started dancing. Even Blackbeard joined us!

When the feast was done, we all fell **asleep**. And the music was replaced by a concert of snores.

ZZZZZZ ZZZZZZ ZZZZZZ

## STOP, THIEF!

We awoke the next morning to loud yelling.

"Stop, thief!"

"The pantry's been ransacked!"

"Someone stole **twenty** steaks, **FORTY** wheels of cheese, and **SIXTY** cheesy buns!"

Benjamin and I *RAN OUT* of our hut as fast as meteorites.

"The pantry is empty," Bart told us. "Someone **stole** all the food!"

The **PIRATES** wandered around the huts looking for tracks, but there were no

**PAWPRINTS** on the ground.

"Hmm, there's nothing here," I observed. "Just **cheese crumbs** and lots of stones."

Captain Blackbeard's eyes lit up. "**What did you say?**" he bellowed.

I almost **JUMPED** out of my fur! "I said, there's nothing —" I began, but he interrupted me.

"**No! What did you say after that?**" he boomed.

"I . . . I said that there were only stones —" I replied.

"**No! Before that! What did you say before that?**"

My ears were ringing — that rodent had quite a voice!

I yelled back. "I SAID THAT THERE ARE ONLY CHEESE CRUMBS ON THE GROUND!"

Blackbeard elbowed me, almost knocking me over.

"Bravo! You found a trail! Let's follow it!"

The cheese crumbs zigged and zagged across the village.

STRANGE!

The thief didn't seem to care that he was leaving a trail.

## VERY STRANGE!

The cheese crumbs led right up to a table. And sitting at the table, sleeping, was Trap!

## EXTREMELY STRANGE!

And that wasn't all. There were two pieces of cheese next to Trap!

"**Here is the thief!**" bellowed Blackbeard.

"*Mmmmff . . . five more minutes*," Trap mumbled sleepily.

Benjamin sighed. "There's only one way to wake up Uncle Trap when he's **sleeping** like this," he said.

He passed a chunk of *stinky*

**cheese** under Trap's snout. My cousin woke up with a smile.

"Good morning!" he said cheerfully.

"Good morning?" boomed Blackbeard. "There's **NOTHING GOOD** about you, thief!"

Wake up now!

zzZzzz
zzZZzz

"**THIEF?**" Trap asked, confused.

"My grandfather thinks you stole all the food from our pantry," Bart explained.

Trap turned as **PALE** as mozzarella. "That's impossible! I was sleeping!" he protested.

"**Uncle Trap is innocent!**" defended Benjamin. "He loves to eat, but he isn't a thief."

Captain Blackbeard shook his head.

# "THIS TRAIL OF CRUMBS IS PROOF! HE IS NO FRIEND OF OURS.

# PIRATES, CAPTURE HIM!"

The pirates **TIED UP** Trap and carried him to their jail hut.

# FOSSILIZED FETA! NOW WHAT???

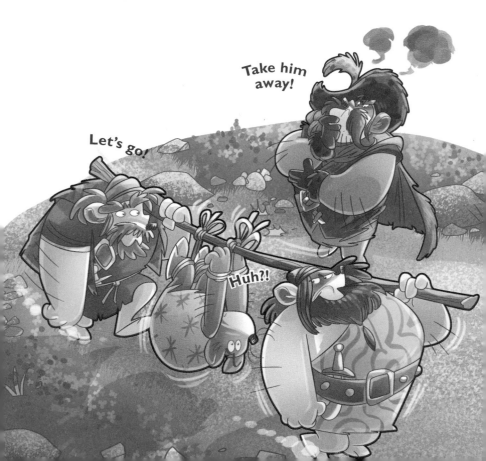

# HOLD ON, TRAP!

Trap gave me a panicked look as he was being carried away.

POOR TRAP! I had never seen him so frightened!

"Cousin, do something!" he pleaded. "Convince them that I am innocent!"

"Don't be scared, Trap! Leave it to me," I promised.

So I went to Captain Blackbeard and took a deep breath. "My cousin is an HONEST RODENT! He isn't a thief. It couldn't have been him!" I said bravely.

"THE TRAIL SPEAKS CLEARLY, GERONIMO!"

he boomed.

The pirate captain was convinced that Trap was guilty.

"To pay for his crime, Trap must work in our village kitchen," Blackbeard announced. "He must spend his days washing dishes. And we will put him on a diet of water and dry bread!"

At these words, Trap fainted. WATER AND DRY BREAD? But he has the appetite of a T. rex!

"There must be some way to prove that Trap is innocent," Thea said.

"BUT WHO COULD it HAVE BEEN?" Bart wondered. "Last night we all fell sound asleep after the party."

"Maybe someone only pretended to

sleep," I suggested.

"Or maybe someone landed on the island during the **NIGHT**," Benjamin chimed in.

Pant ... pant!

"Of course!" Thea cried. She took my arm and **dragged** me toward the beach. Bart and Benjamin followed us.

We soon came across **Spotty**, who looked hot and miserable.

We quickly found out why. The sand under our paws was **sizzling** hot!

Spotty flopped over on his belly and slid toward the sea at *SUPER SPEED*.

"I have an idea!" Bart cried. He grabbed a big palm frond, sat on it, and started

*SLIDING* after Spotty.

"Come on, Uncle G!" Benjamin cried. "This is fun!"

I couldn't say no to my nephew. I HOPPED onto the leaf behind him and then . . .

VROOOOOOOOOOOOOOM!

We **HURTLED** toward the beach like lightning! Thea zipped down alongside us.

"Are there any **brakes** on this leaf?" I yelled, but of course there weren't. We had no choice but to CRASH-LAND into the soft sand on the shore.

Thea JUMPED UP first and ran onto the *Speedy Cheddar 3*. We followed her.

"LOOK! The pantry is even emptier than before!" she exclaimed. "And look at the deck! It's full of the remains of a feast. Cheese rinds, bread crumbs, and **HALF-EATEN** steaks!"

# HOW STRANGE!

"So this means that Uncle Trap was right!" Benjamin said. "We thought that he had RAIDED the pantry during our voyage. But . . ."

"Someone must have SECRETLY come on board!" Thea finished.

"But who could it be?" Bart wondered.

And then it came to me. I knew who the **REAL THIEVES** were! I quickly came up with a plan.

It had to work — for Trap!

I know!

# A TRAP TO HELP TRAP!

A few hours later, Bart went to Blackbeard and told him that we could not **prove** that Trap was innocent.

"Then Trap is **guilty**!" Blackbeard boomed. "Let us hold a **fEAST** and put this unpleasantness behind us. We will use our emergency supplies."

"Huzzah! A party!" cheered the pirates.

But poor Trap was not cheering. First he had to **wash** all the dirty pots and dishes from yesterday's banquet. He scrubbed and scrubbed. **1**

Then he had to **sweep** the entire village **2** and **polish** the swords of all the **PREHISTORIC PIRATES**!  3

I approached him right before the banquet began.

"Cousin, you've got to **HELP ME**!" Trap pleaded. "I have never worked so hard in my life!"

"Hang in there," I whispered to him. "We have a **plan**!"

"How long do I have to wait?" Trap asked. "I'm working my poor 🐾 P A W S 🐾 off! And my tummy is so EMPTY." He

rubbed it, and it growled.

"You'll be **FREE** before the night is over," I promised.

And then the feast began, and the pirates ate and sang and danced like they had the night before. Exhausted, the pirates fell sound asleep.

Thea, Bart, Benjamin, and I only pretended to sleep. We were keeping an eye on the pantry, which still had some food left in it.

Suddenly, we saw two dark shadows approach.

These weren't just any shadows. They were SABER-TOOTHED TIGERS!

I flashed back to that night in Old Mouse City before we sailed off. I was sure I had seen tigers that night. Now it all made sense!

Those rotten felines had stowed away in the *Speedy Cheddar 3*! They had sailed with

us for days and days. My fur **BRISTLED** in fear at the thought of it.

Those tigers had been *SNEAKY*. But now it was our turn to sneak up on them. As soon as they tiptoed out of the pantry, we pelted them with **coconuts**!

# BONK! BONK! BONK!

We pummeled them from the tops of their heads to the tips of their tails!

This megalithic **RACKET** woke up Blackbeard and the prehistoric pirates, who dashed to the pantry.

"**WHAT IS GOING ON HERE?**" yelled Captain Blackbeard angrily.

But as soon as the pirates saw the fierce saber-toothed tigers, they **froze** in fear. And we were out of coconuts! The tigers started to **ROAR** and snarl, threatening us with their fangs and CLAWS.

"**GROWL!** We will eat you up!" threatened one.

"**MEEEEOW!** We will serve you **stewed** with a side of Jurassic onions!" said the other.

Squeak! How scary!

The once-tough PIRATES were all trembling with fear — all except for Blackbeard Barnacle. He stayed very **calm**.

"Roooaaar!" growled the first tiger.

Blackbeard just yawned. "Is that all you've got?" he asked.

"**ROOOAAAR!**" growled the second tiger.

"Are you **finished** yet?" Blackbeard asked calmly.

He didn't wait for an answer. He brought his paw to his mouth and whistled.

# TWEEEEEET!

A second later, the ground began to **shake**. A huge creature slid into the village. It was **Spotty**, the walrusaurus guardian of Black Rock Island!

Seeing his friends in **DANGER**, he launched himself at the tigers. He sat right on top of them, **PINNING THEM DOWN** with his fins!

Oompf!

**"LET US GO!"** shrieked the tigers. Now it was their turn to be terrified!

"Let you go?" I cried out as **bravely** as I could. "Absolutely not! Unless you want to be Spotty's lunch, you must tell the truth."

Being so close to these terrifying tigers was making my heart beat like a **DRUM**. But I had to save Trap.

"What truth? We haven't done anything wrong," said one of the tigers.

"Did you **stow away** on our ship?" asked Thea.

"**NO, NO, NO!** Absolutely not!" the tigers protested.

Bart nodded to Spotty. "Enjoy your meal."

The tigers looked up at Spotty's **HUGE TUSKS** and quickly changed their story.

"Tiger Khan asked us to go to Old Mouse City and **KIDNAP** Bart Barnacle," one of them said.

"And then **RANSOM** him for the

treasure of the prehistoric pirates," finished the second.

"But the chubby mouse saw us inside the tavern . . ."

"And we dove into the water to escape!"

"**And we hate water!**" the two tigers exclaimed together. "We swam to your ship and hid aboard."

"So it was you who stole the food on the ship and here in the village?" I asked.

They nodded. "**Yes! It was us!**"

Captain Blackbeard marched over to Trap.

**"YOU ARE FREE! THE PREHISTORIC PIRATES ASK FOR YOUR FORGIVENESS!"** he bellowed.

Then he clapped his paws. "**Another Feast!**"

I couldn't believe it. We hadn't had so many

parties since Grandma Ratrock's birthday!

While the pirates **CHEERED**, the tigers slid out from under Spotty. But before they could scurry away, Spotty whacked them with his fin. He sent them **FLYING** into the sea.

SPLASH!

Benjamin and I hugged the walrusaurus. He was a true hero!

Arf . . . Arf!

Thank you!

# GOOD-BYE, FRIENDS!

With the help of Bart Barnacle and the prehistoric pirates, we **REPAIRED** the *Speedy Cheddar 3* and prepared to return home.

Our friends filled the **galley**\* with enough cheeses, tropical fruits, and treats to last the *long voyage*. This time, we would be sailing without Bart as our captain. But thanks to his **TRAINING**, we knew what to do. Thea took the wheel. Benjamin and I **scurried** up the mast to set the sails. And Trap helped by organizing the **food**, of course!

\*The galley of a ship is the kitchen.

When the ship was **READY** to go, Bart and his grandfather Blackbeard Barnacle came aboard to say good-bye.

"IT WAS AN HONOR FOR THE PREHISTORIC PIRATES TO MEET YOU, FRIENDS!"

Blackbeard roared. "**WE HOPE TO SEE YOU SOON!**"

Then he hugged me tightly. I could hear my **BONES** cracking under his grasp! On shore, all the prehistoric pirates CHEERED and waved.

Then it was Bart's turn. He hugged each one of us (more gently than his grandfather had, thank goodmouse). Then he gave us a chest filled with **shells**, enormouse pearls, sparkling **emeralds**, and other fabumouse pirate jewels!

Bouncing boulders, what a mousetastic surprise! If the saber-toothed tigers had seen this, they would have pulled out their whiskers with JEALOUSY!

"Thank you, my friend," I said, shaking his paw. "We will miss you!"

"But our paths will cross again," Bart replied with a WINK. "A pirate never stays in one place for long! I'm sure I'll soon set sail on another adventure and see you again."

"In *Old Mouse City*, I hope!" I said with a sigh.

Black Rock Island was **beautiful**, but I really wanted to go **home**.

"I will return to your city," Bart promised. "It's not every day a mouse meets **friends** like you!"

Then Bart and Blackbeard headed back to shore. **Spotty** helped push us out to sea while the prehistoric pirates **happily** waved good-bye from the beach. With Thea at the helm, the sails swelled, and we glided away through the **waves** toward Old Mouse City.

"I'm sorry this **VACATION** is over," Trap remarked.

"Vacation? The pirates made you do all that work!" I reminded him.

"Yes, all that work was terrible, but those

feasts!" Trap got a *dreamy* look in his eyes. "So much food!"

"Well, there's **food** waiting for you at the Rotten Tooth Tavern," I pointed out.

"This was a great trip!" Thea chimed in. "I'm glad I learned how to sail a ship."

"And I'm glad I learned that I'm a great singer," Trap said. He grabbed his mandolin and began to strum and sing.

> **"Let's sail back quickly**
> **on the ocean breeze,**
> **So we can get home and**
> **eat some more cheese!"**

Bones and stones, his singing was TORTURE!

I plugged my ears and sighed. I almost preferred the danger of saber-toothed tigers

to this. Almost! My cousin's singing was **terrible** . . . but maybe it would keep away the sea monsters!

And that's the truth, or I'm not . . .

# Don't miss any adventures of the cavemice!

#1 The Stone of Fire

#2 Watch Your Tail!

#3 Help, I'm in Hot Lava!

#4 The Fast and the Frozen

#5 The Great Mouse Race

#6 Don't Wake the Dinosaur!

#7 I'm a Scaredy-Mouse!

#8 Surfing for Secrets

#9 Get the Scoop, Geronimo!

#10 My Autosaurus Will Win!

#11 Sea Monster Surprise

Up Next!

#12 Paws Off the Pearl!

# Be sure to read all my fabumouse adventures!

#1 Lost Treasure of the Emerald Eye

#2 The Curse of the Cheese Pyramid

#3 Cat and Mouse in a Haunted House

#4 I'm Too Fond of My Fur!

#5 Four Mice Deep in the Jungle

#6 Paws Off, Cheddarface!

#7 Red Pizzas for a Blue Count

#8 Attack of the Bandit Cats

#9 A Fabumouse Vacation for Geronimo

#10 All Because of a Cup of Coffee

#11 It's Halloween, You 'Fraidy Mouse!

#12 Merry Christmas, Geronimo!

#13 The Phantom of the Subway

#14 The Temple of the Ruby of Fire

#15 The Mona Mousa Code

#16 A Cheese-Colored Camper

#17 Watch Your Whiskers, Stilton!

#18 Shipwreck on the Pirate Islands

#19 My Name Is Stilton, Geronimo Stilton

#20 Surf's Up, Geronimo!

**#21 The Wild, Wild West**

**#22 The Secret of Cacklefur Castle**

**A Christmas Tale**

**#23 Valentine's Day Disaster**

**#24 Field Trip to Niagara Falls**

**#25 The Search for Sunken Treasure**

**#26 The Mummy with No Name**

**#27 The Christmas Toy Factory**

**#28 Wedding Crasher**

**#29 Down and Out Down Under**

**#30 The Mouse Island Marathon**

**#31 The Mysterious Cheese Thief**

**Christmas Catastrophe**

**#32 Valley of the Giant Skeletons**

**#33 Geronimo and the Gold Medal Mystery**

**#34 Geronimo Stilton, Secret Agent**

**#35 A Very Merry Christmas**

**#36 Geronimo's Valentine**

**#37 The Race Across America**

**#38 A Fabumouse School Adventure**

**#39 Singing Sensation**

**#40 The Karate Mouse**

**#41 Mighty Mount Kilimanjaro**

**#42 The Peculiar Pumpkin Thief**

**#43 I'm Not a Supermouse!**

#44 The Giant Diamond Robbery

#45 Save the White Whale!

#46 The Haunted Castle

#47 Run for the Hills, Geronimo!

#48 The Mystery in Venice

#49 The Way of the Samurai

#50 This Hotel Is Haunted!

#51 The Enormouse Pearl Heist

#52 Mouse in Space!

#53 Rumble in the Jungle

#54 Get into Gear, Stilton!

#55 The Golden Statue Plot

#56 Flight of the Red Bandit

The Hunt for the Golden Book

#57 The Stinky Cheese Vacation

#58 The Super Chef Contest

#59 Welcome to Moldy Manor

The Hunt for the Curious Cheese

#60 The Treasure of Easter Island

#61 Mouse House Hunter

#62 Mouse Overboard!

The Hunt for the Secret Papyrus

#63 The Cheese Experiment

#64 Magical Mission

# MEET
# Geronimo Stiltonord

He is a mouseking — the Geronimo Stilton of the ancient far north! He lives with his brawny and brave clan in the village of Mouseborg. From sailing frozen waters to facing fiery dragons, every day is an adventure for the micekings!

#1 Attack of the Dragons

#2 The Famouse Fjord Race

#3 Pull the Dragon's Tooth!

# MEET
# GERONIMO STILTONIX

He is a spacemouse — the Geronimo Stilton of a parallel universe! He is captain of the spaceship *MouseStar 1*. While flying through the cosmos, he visits distant planets and meets crazy aliens. His adventures are out of this world!

#1 Alien Escape

#2 You're Mine, Captain!

#3 Ice Planet Adventure

#4 The Galactic Goal

#5 Rescue Rebellion

#6 The Underwater Planet

#7 Beware! Space Junk!

#8 Away in a Star Sled

CHEDDAR VOLCANO

SINGING ROCK SQUARE

EFTYMOUSE HOUSE

HOSPITAL

FLIGHTPORT

SUBWAYSAURUS STATION

THEA'S HOUSE

GRANDMA RATROCK'S HOUSE

GERONIMO'S HOUSE

THE SHAMAN'S GROTTO

DEAR MOUSE FRIENDS,
THANKS FOR READING,
AND GOOD-BYE UNTIL
THE NEXT BOOK!